A New Year's Tale

Translated by Max Hayward
Decorations by William McLaren

By Vladimir Dudintsev

NOT BY BREAD ALONE

A New Year's Tale

VLADIMIR DUDINTSEV

HUTCHINSON OF LONDON

HUTCHINSON & CO. (*Publishers*) LTD
178-202 Great Portland Street, London, W.1

London Melbourne Sydney
Auckland Bombay Toronto
Johannesburg New York

★

First published 1960

*This book has been set in Spectrum type face. It has
been printed in Great Britain by The Anchor Press,
Ltd., in Tiptree, Essex, on Ant Laid paper and
bound by Taylor Garnett Evans & Co., Ltd., in
Watford, Herts*

Translator's Preface

It is now four years since Vladimir Dudintsev caused a sensation both in his own country and abroad by publishing his novel *Not by Bread Alone* in the literary monthly *Novy Mir*. The Soviet literary 'establishment' reacted with fury. In the very unfavourable atmosphere that followed the Hungarian revolution the bureaucrats who then controlled the Union of Writers were able to play on the apprehensions of the Party that too much freedom for intellectuals might lead to the same breakdown of its authority as had taken place in Poland and Hungary. Early in 1957 Khrushchev himself angrily called the writers to heel. In tones ominously reminiscent of Zhdanov he reminded them that nobody could call himself a Soviet writer unless he was prepared to accept the 'guidance' of the Party unconditionally. It looked for a time as though all the gains which Soviet writers had made since Stalin's death might be wiped out. Dudintsev and others like him were hounded into silence by critics pretending to speak in the name of outraged public opinion. One of the most unpleasant and sinister contributions to the campaign against them was an officially boosted novel by V. Kochetov, *The Brothers Ershov*, in which it was suggested that intellectual disobedience was tantamount to high treason and that the rebellious Hungarian intellectuals had been morally responsible for the hanging of 'communists' from the lamp-posts of Budapest.

Dudintsev was particularly vulnerable in this campaign; he had gone further than anybody in the demand for greater intellectual freedom. *Not by Bread Alone* was a manifesto. It enraged its critics not so much because of its frank exposure of bureaucratic abuse in Soviet society (this, within limits, has always been a permissible target) as because of its powerful plea for intellectual honesty. This was something explosively new in Soviet literature. Lopatkin, the hero of the novel, is a lone rebel who fights for the truth as he sees it, not as the authorities will it. In thus raising the individual and his conscience above the cowardly and conservative 'collective', Dudintsev was upsetting the Socialist Realist axiom that the way to success and glory lies through service to a higher truth mysteriously invested in the Party as the spokesman of the masses. To make matters worse he even exploited 'orthodox' symbols in defence of individual responsibility. The word 'communism', for example, is subtly redefined by Lopatkin as devoted service to a personal, yet unselfish ideal:

'When I realized the importance of this machine [the invention Lopatkin is vainly trying to get accepted by the authorities] and understood that I should have to tighten my belt for the sake of it, I didn't hesitate for one second and gladly plunged into the whirlpool. . . . And now I have suddenly realized that *Communism is not a scheme invented by philosophers, but a force that has existed for a very long time* and which is gradually preparing cadres for the society of the future. . . .'

The hero of *A New Year's Tale*, which was published

6

in *Novy Mir* in January of this year, shares this ascetic idealism of Lopatkin. Like Lopatkin he is an inventor who eventually triumphs by stubbornly following his personal vision. Dudintsev has thus reasserted the 'heresy' for which he was so savagely attacked four years ago. He has, furthermore, chosen to express it in an allegorical form which, with all its ambiguities, would have been quite unthinkable at that time. 'Academician S.' and the 'personnel officer', for instance, patently refer to the type of hide-bound conformists who persecuted and silenced the author after the publication of *Not by Bread Alone*. The 'reformed bandit', as some commentators have suggested, may well be partly inspired by the idea of Mr. Khrushchev as an anti-Stalinist crusader. If this is so—and the curious parallel between Khrushchev's 'secret speech' to the 20th Congress and the letter which the bandit writes to the 'Brotherhood' suggests that it is—then the Fable is to some extent an expression of faith in Khrushchev. Dudintsev certainly has every reason to be grateful to him, for it was Khrushchev, speaking at the 3rd Congress of Soviet Writers in May 1959, who defended Dudintsev against his critics and thoroughly discomfited them by announcing that *Not by Bread Alone* was one of the few books he had read without having to prick himself with a pin to keep awake. This does not, of course, mean that Khrushchev is now a champion of unbridled freedom for intellectuals, but his speech at the Writers' Congress showed his understanding of the fact that writers, like kolkhozniks, are able and willing to produce only if they are allowed some scope in running their own affairs. The persecution of Dudintsev and others in 1956 resulted in a 'conspiracy of silence' on the part of most leading writers. This was the only way in which they could protest. When the Party had recovered from its fright over Hungary they were able to fight back in other ways too, and by 1959 the diehards (the sort of people represented by 'Academician S.' and the 'personnel officer' in the Fable) were clearly on the defensive. By not supporting the diehards and their methods at the Writers' Congress, Khrushchev tipped the balance against them and they lost their commanding position in the apparatus of the Union of Writers. The new secretariat included Alexander Tvardovsky, the editor of *Novy Mir* and, hence, Dudintsev's publisher.

Perhaps the most significant point about the Tale, then, is that its publication demonstrates the enormous improvement in the situation of Soviet writers since last year. For the first time in decades a 'controversial' work has been published without provoking a sordid campaign of denunciation and vilification. The Fable *New Year's Tale* has been calmly accepted and there has been no outcry from any quarter.

MAX HAYWARD

1

I LIVE in a fantastic world, a legendary country, in a city created by my imagination. Amazing things happen to people in it, and I have had my share of such adventures. Taking advantage of this New Year season, when people readily believe unlikely tales, I'll tell you some of them. I am concerned with time and the tricks it plays on us. Time, as you know, is infinite and ubiquitous. In my imaginary world you can set your watch by Moscow time, and this is why I venture to begin my story; there may be readers who will find that parts of it impinge upon their own, real, earnest lives.

A mysterious bird, an owl, has flown into our town. Several people have received visits from it. The first was my immediate boss, the head of a team of scientists who are studying the sun. The second was my old school friend, now a specialist in nervous diseases; the third was myself. It's a remarkable bird. It is a pity that its habits are not studied and that there is no picture of it in the textbooks.

By the time it came I had already published several works on the properties of sunlight. I had a degree, I sat as a consultant on several commissions, and I was in a hurry to become established and respectable. After the manner of our grand old men, I held my chin up and whenever I was asked a question took my time before delivering a weighty, well-thought-out reply in a well-modulated voice. I also took good care of my expensive coat. Our rooms have cupboards and, like the older men, I kept in mine a hanger marked with my initials.

Endowed with talents, however modest, I followed the advice of an Academician and trained myself to put down such stray thoughts as came into my head. For, of course, the most fruitful thoughts are not those we sweat out of ourselves, sitting at a desk for hours, but those that blow in like a gust of wind, most often as we stroll along the street. I would make a note and forget all about it. But our charwoman kept in mind the scraps of paper, as inflammable as dynamite, which filled my drawers, and took to clearing out my desk and using them to light our stoves.

Beneath the shell of my respectability I was as ingenuous as a child (so, incidentally, was our head). At times the child with chubby cheeks came into the open, particularly during those evening hours which several of us unmarried men spent in our common living room before the television set, round-eyed and as motionless as specimens preserved in spirits, watching the legs of football-players flitting over the bluish screen.

As you see, I spare no one and myself least of all. I consciously reveal, and will continue to reveal and to submit to you for judgement, many aspects of my character which I am myself the first to judge. It is as if my eyes had recently been opened; to be exact, it happened the day the owl visited me for the first time. It was the owl that opened them and I am grateful to it.

To take one example, I could now see my quarrel with S in a completely new light. S is a corresponding member in a provincial academy of sciences. In an article he wrote five years ago he called a well-known published work of mine 'the fruit of idle speculation'. I had to reply. In my own article I refuted S's arguments as though by the way, and got in the following words which I thought were very telling: 'This is exactly what Dr. S is trying so unsuccessfully to prove.' (I knew that although he was a corresponding member he was not a full Academician but merely a Doctor of Science like myself.) S immediately produced a monograph in which, equally by the way, he accused me of forcing the results of my experiments to prove my 'theory' (theory in inverted commas). Soon after this I published a long article on my most recent observations of the sun; these confirmed my theory and made mincemeat of S. 'Battleship torpedoed amidships,' said my colleagues. Assuming that he would be completely sunk, I had not referred to S by name but only mentioned 'certain authors'. The battleship, however, survived and returned my fire. . . .

And so on. . . . Five years of these hostilities had shattered my nerves, and not only mine.

But to come back to my story: one morning we had all gathered at the laboratory, hung our coats up on their hangers, and, before getting down to work, settled to our usual morning chat. It was begun by our respected Director. He devoted his spare time to collecting books, stone axe-heads, coins, and generally to the study of antiquity; it seemed to me, indeed, that this hobby, more than our research, gave purpose to his uneventful life.

'Here's an odd thing,' he said to us. 'The other day I was reading an inscription on a tombstone and I found this curious emblem engraved on it.'

He showed us a sheet of paper on which an owl was drawn in Indian ink.

'I managed to decipher the inscription too,' he said with pride. 'There was a name followed by the words: "And he lived nine hundred years." '

'Well, well,' said one of us, a man of wit and fashion, with a far-away look. 'I'd even settle for four hundred.'

'Whatever for?' another colleague asked sharply. He was a lean, broad-shouldered, middle-aged man who sat next to me and who usually remained silent. He differed from the rest of us by his neglected clothes, his taciturnity, and his unbelievable capacity for work. 'You don't need four hundred years. You're in no hurry as it is.'

'May I point out,' the Director raised his voice, letting it be understood that we had interrupted him. 'May I point out that owls of this variety have been found at different times in widely scattered countries. There is even an enormous granite carving of an owl standing in a desert. But in our region this is the first ever to have been found. If I may say so without boasting,' he beamed, 'both the inscription and the owl are my own discovery. I happened to dig up the tombstone in my garden.'

We all congratulated him on his luck, had another look at the owl, and went to our places.

'I am determined to find out the meaning of this

emblem,' said the Director. 'Then I might publish something.'

'Could it have been a hieroglyph to denote a man who knew how to use his time?' I suggested.

'Possibly. But it would still have to be proved.'

'All the same, nine hundred years!' I couldn't help exclaiming. 'Do you think it's possible that there were ever people who lived as long as that?'

'Everything is possible,' grunted my industrious neighbour without looking up.

'What do you mean by that?' the Director asked politely.

'Time is an enigma,' he replied more enigmatically still.

'Yes, that's true.' The Director seized on the idea with interest. Taking down an hour-glass from its bracket on the wall, he turned it over, put it on the desk in front of him, and watched the sand. 'See how strange! the instant we are living through is like the smallest grain of sand—less than that: a mathematical point. . . . It's already gone.'

I felt a sudden stab of pain. I had once had several months of an amazing, unexpected love, and now these months, as I looked back on them in sorrow, merged into a single moment and become a grain of sand which had slipped away. Not a trace was left— as if these months had never been! I sighed. If only the glass could be turned back upside-down!

The voice of our personnel officer broke in on my thoughts: 'May I ask you, Chief? According to your theory—if you can call it that—time is a mathematical point. Then what becomes of our heroic past? And what about our radiant future?'

He liked asking forthright questions in a loud voice, as though making some frightful accusation.

'I'm sorry if I have put it badly,' said the chief, who was a peace-loving man. 'But I didn't think I had got round to formulating any theory. I was only joking, speculating. . . .'

'Odd sort of speculation. There are limits, after all . . .'

'My dear man,' grunted our dishevelled and hard-working eccentric so loudly that we all turned round. 'The kind of new thing we are looking for is nearly always beyond the limit'; and, opening his mouth in a way he had, he laughed silently into the other's pursed-up face. Thus he revealed to us a new side of his character.

For two years we had sat in the same room, yet how little had we learnt about him! All we saw was that he rarely shaved, and that he dumped his coat on the back of his chair. We had also noticed that half the buttons on the coat were missing, and finally that he did four men's work. But not one of us had really got to know him.

'You know, I'd like to tell you of an interesting case,' he spoke again, still bending over his work.

That he should waste his time on talking to us amazed us: he had never yet been guilty of such extravagance. Who'd have thought that our discussion of longevity would have stirred him up so much?

'I'll just run down to the basement and set up my apparatus, not to waste time. I won't be a moment.' He hurried out.

'Is he a dry old stick or isn't he?' one of us asked.

'I don't think he is,' said our man-about-town. 'You know, I live next door to him. There is a woman who comes to see him. Can you believe it—a young woman!

I bumped into her once—there she was, going up the stairs, blind to everything. Dazzled by love.'

'You know, he has a very rare old watch. It's extremely accurate and it needs winding up only once a year,' said the Director.

'Well now, my friends.' Grey, dishevelled, our new friend (we hadn't really met him until today) came back and sat down at his desk, holding a slide-rule. 'Nine hundred years, you said. . . . But you know that time can stand still and can also fly. Have you ever waited for a girl you love?'

'Yes,' said the boss, 'time can be very slow.'

'It can stand still. Do you remember reading about those scientists who found some lotus seeds in a two-thousand-year-old tomb and made them grow? For those seeds time had stood still. Time can be slowed down or given a push.' He made a measurement with his slide-rule and wrote it down; he managed to work even while he talked.

'The story I'm going to tell you illustrates this point. You'll find it interesting, quite apart from its message.'

He turned to me (or so I thought) as if his words were meant for me alone.

'Once upon a time, in a far-away kingdom—to be more exact, a few years ago in this very town—this is what happened. One Sunday, some sixty, or perhaps a hundred, well-dressed men gathered in a secluded, shady spot in the Park of Culture for an open-air discussion. Later on it was discovered that this two-hour session in our park had been a—what shall I call it—a symposium of thieves and bandits, members of a so-called "Brotherhood". Such people have their own strict rules; the punishment for breaking them is death. A new member has to have two sponsors, and when he joins a few words are tattooed on his chest—a motto by which it can be known that he belongs.'

'What is the connection between your story and our discussion about time?' the boss asked gently. 'Or perhaps you haven't finished?'

'No, I haven't. It couldn't be a closer connection. I'm coming to it. . . . At the congress of the bandits six sentences of death were passed. Five of them have been carried out. The sixth man is still at large owing to certain complications. But I must tell you who he is and what he had done wrong. This man was the head, the president, or, as they say, the "Gaffer" of the whole "Brotherhood", the oldest and the most cunning of the bandits. He had been put in prison in some out-of-the-way place, and it must have been while he was there, sitting in solitary, that it occurred to him that he had never done anything in his life or got anything out of it, and that now he hadn't long to live. His reasoning was this: the whole point of a bandit's life is the acquisition, by the easiest possible means, of other people's property, such things as gold and other valuables. But the value and importance of riches in human society were deteriorating at a catastrophic pace.'

'Quite a theoretician your bandit seems to be,' the personnel officer said ironically.

'Yes, he was a man who meant business,' agreed our eccentric. I liked him more and more all the time. 'In recent years this criminal, who had done so much harm, had sobered up and taken to reading. Books, as you know, have enormous power. He had got through lots of them. He was in no hurry to be released—it suited him to read and think sitting in his stone box—and as he was their chief the bandits smuggled in whatever book he wanted, even if it was kept under lock and key inside the vaults of the State Treasury. Yes, well . . . So he realized that things were losing their prestige at a catastrophic pace. Once upon a time princes and rich men used to breed morey eels in pools specially constructed inside lagoons. The eels were fed on the flesh of slaves. Such an eel served at a dinner party was regarded as the greatest of delicacies. And yet now we can't think without a shudder about these pastimes of our ancestors. There was a time when gold was a nameless metal slumbering in the earth. Later, man gave it a value and a name. Gold glittering on clothes or weapons came to be regarded as the height of elegance. Yet not one of us today would venture out with a gold chain stretched across his stomach or even with a gold pin in his tie. Gold is losing its prestige. And what of the prestige of precious stuffs? I can assure you that at this very moment costly fabrics are going out of fashion never to return. To show off rich possessions nowadays is a sign of spiritual backwardness.'

'Fancy that! So your bandit has written off all material values. And what's to take the place of things, I'd like to know?' said the personnel officer. He felt put out, for it so happened that he fancied himself in expensive tweeds with padded shoulders and his wife had once called for him at the laboratory with a splendid silver fox over her arm.

'It depends what things you mean. There are things and things. This is just what the bandit had observed, and it made him think. He realized that the adulation of material things was being ineluctably defeated by the beauty of the human soul, beauty which can neither be bought nor stolen. You can't make anyone love you by force of arms. The beauty of the soul is free and it took pride of place the moment gold and velvet gave up their positions. So now a Cinderella in a cotton print can outshine a princess draped in satin. Because what gives its value to a cheap dress is the beauty of its cut and design, which is no longer a material value. It's the result of taste and character in those who thought of it, or chose to wear it. No wonder that nowadays many princesses who have kept their souls dress up as Cinderellas. And if we do come across a woman hung with furs and precious stuffs, instead of being dazzled by her display of wealth, we shy away as from a spiritual cripple who is parading her deformity.

'This is what my bandit had observed, and suddenly he realized that never in all his life had he possessed such "things" as the approval of his fellow men, or friendship, or true love—all his life he had spent chasing after things which had no value. Something like a currency reform took place in him. Yes. . . .' The speaker cleared his voice. 'And yet people whose love and friendship he so much needed did exist. He knew of them. . . . There was a woman . . . But he couldn't even face her. He couldn't come into the open, it was too risky.

'Eventually he put down all his ideas in a long letter to the "Brotherhood", saying that he was resigning his "office" and joining the society of normal people who work for their living, and adding that he intended to achieve by some outstanding action what he had never yet experienced in life but now longed for with all his being. The prison administration had his letter printed as a leaflet. You realize, of course, that it was a document of great power; it was important to make use of it.

'Now look at the situation in which the "Gaffer"

found himself. In the course of his life he had been sentenced by various courts to prison terms amounting to some two hundred years. He knew that the State would not remit his punishment. On the other hand, knowing the rules and customs of the "Brotherhood" better than anyone, he realized that they would not forgive him for his betrayal and that somewhere a knife was being sharpened for him. But he needed at least a few more years of life in order to carry out his plan. So before the "Brotherhood" had passed sentence he made his last jail-break. He had plenty of money and he found clever doctors who worked a transformation on him, just as in a fairy tale; they grafted new skin on his face and hands and changed his hair; they even changed his voice. They were first-class experts.

'He got hold of new, immaculate identity papers and became a new man. In three years he graduated from two universities and, at the moment, he is completing his work, which is enormous in conception. He wants to make a gift to his fellow men——'

'That's all very well,' I interrupted him, because he kept his eyes fixed steadily upon me. 'But what has any of this to do with our discussion—with time standing still or flying, or the inscription: "He lived nine hundred years"?'

'It has everything to do with it. Here is a man hunted by his executioners. They dog his footsteps and they will inevitably catch up with him. He has very little time left. *Time*—you see what I mean? And this man is determined to live the whole of his life over again within the span of a couple of years. But suppose he had lived all his life as he is living now? He might well have lived nine hundred years and more.'

'You are speaking, of course, about the content of his life and not its length?' said the chief.

'It's obvious *you* don't economize your time!' My neighbour lost his temper. 'Yes, yes, yes! Content! What we fill the vessel of time with. It should be filled only with the greatest joys, the most powerful sensations of delight we can experience. . . .'

'Now you've let your hair down,' said the personnel officer. 'So you are preaching pure selfishness! All you want are joys, delights! And what about the little matter of working for the people? What d'you think of that? Eh?'

'What I think is that you're behind the times. You should be taken in tow. You imagine that joy is a sin —the sin you secretly indulge in within the privacy of your four walls—and that working for the people is just your public duty. Compared with you my bandit is a man of advanced views. He has tested all your joys and he is sick and tired of them. There's only one joy he believes in now, and that's what you regard as a grim duty.'

'Tell me,' said the boss after a moment's silence, 'how do you know all these details? Here's a man who has changed his face, his name . . . and he's surely not a fool—I can't see him confiding in strangers.'

'I'm not a stranger to him.'

'You should give him up to the authorities if you know your duty as a citizen,' the personnel officer said abruptly. 'You should report him—a man who has committed so many crimes and has escaped from prison. . . .'

'Not on your life,' said our colleague. 'Not on your life. He is not a bandit now. He's harmless, he's even useful. When he's done his job he'll give himself up.'

He reached into his pocket for his famous watch—a heavy, round, old-fashioned watch on a steel chain.

'Sorry. I've got to go and check my instruments.'

He stopped on his way out.

'You ought to think about my story. You particularly,' he looked me straight in the eyes. 'You might consider the experience of others and stop playing with trifles. I'm thinking about your squabble with the corresponding member. . . .'

How could I suppose then that I was to be drawn into his story, play the hero's part in it, become the hero's double?

2

A BOUT half an hour later I followed him into the basement; I wanted to check on a suspicion which had suddenly arisen in my mind. There he sat surrounded by the gleam of glass and copper. The door scarcely creaked, but he ducked so suddenly that he knocked over several test-tubes.

'Sorry,' I said.

'Checking up on your hunch?' He was regaining his composure.

'You're a bit reckless.'

'I'm not afraid of you.' He turned back to his instruments.

Now that I was sure, I understood the meaning of several other things which I have not so far mentioned.

It had recently become obvious that someone was taking an unaccountable interest in my person. I was being shadowed. Not once did I get a good look at whoever it was who dogged my steps, although in fact he (or she) never hurried out of sight. He (or she) would take up a position in some dark doorway, but would now and then venture boldly out into the sunlight, slipping back only when I reached into my pocket for my spectacles. Several times I went up to the gate or doorway through which my follower, who seemed to be drawn to me, had vanished, only to find it empty. A few days ago there came the first fall of cleanest, softest snow. Late that evening I was walking along a deserted street when I heard footsteps at my back and guessed, before I even turned my head, that this was he (or she). When I did turn round I caught a glimpse of something that might have been a cloak or a tail-coat vanishing down a sidestreet. I hared after it like a madman, but when I reached the corner all I saw was the white, peaceful alleyway and not a soul in sight. I looked down at the snow but there were no footprints. It is true that afterwards I remembered several cross-shaped tracks, rather like those of an enormous hen, melting into the soft, porous snow.

Now, as I stood talking to my colleague in the basement, I told him all about it. He shook my hand and said: 'Thank you. I've noticed a few things myself. Now go. I have to hurry. As you see, I'm very short of time. Incidentally, it wouldn't be a bad idea if you pressed on a little too. You never know what might happen.'

We were both working on the same problem, but we approached it from different angles. One of us was wrong, the other right. But the problem was so important that even a mistake was worth it if it would clear the way for other scientists. We were looking for a method of condensing sunlight. The end result we hoped for would produce months or even years of brilliant light and warmth for a distant continent which never saw the sun. One side of our planet had no sunshine—it lived in perpetual winter and eternal night. The fact that this, the most important of our problems, was the one my colleague had seized upon was to my mind a further proof of his identity: here in front of me was the bandit chief in a hurry to live. Would a year, or even two, suffice him for his task?

I judge things soberly and count my costs. If I was

marking time, year in, year out, wondering which side of the problem to tackle first, it was because to start on my research meant putting other things aside and burying myself in my job for a good ten years. If only the whole team could have been pulled in on the project! But it was something to be allowed to work on it at all. Many people were against it; nearly all the members of the Academic Council thought of us as crackpots. Anyway, there it was—ten years. . . . What could be achieved in two?

As it turned out, he had not two years to live, but only a few more hours. Next morning I was rung up from the hospital. My remarkable bandit had been found in the night, bleeding to death on our door-step (we lived in the same house). He had several deep knife-wounds in the back. The whole Institute was in an uproar. Several well-known specialists were called in, but it was too late. By midday the more active members of the Institute were ringing up the under-takers.

His death, and the fact that he had seemingly fore-told it, was a profound shock to us. For several days we exchanged meaningful glances whenever we all met. My nerves went to pieces. I panicked and lost weight. I couldn't bear to listen to any talk unless it was related to the job and I worked intensively for a week. After that I received the current number of our periodical, saw that S was one of the contributors, and got so excited that everything except that printed page went clean out of my head. I leafed nervously through the journal and caught sight of a footnote (the worst insults are always set in small print). There, among polite but deadly words, I found my name. I did another somersault and settled back into my old groove. Paper! Paper! Who was it who invented you?

I gave up work and, urged by my supporters, wrote an article with not just one, but three footnotes intended finally to make an end of S; the whole team took part in drafting them. And if you want a picture of us concentrating on this work, I suggest that you should go to the Tretyakov Gallery and look at Repin's *Zaporozhian Cossacks*. There we all are, including the boss, splitting his sides with laughter, and myself sitting at the desk, bespectacled and pen in hand.

Once I was on my old familiar track I quite forgot the watcher who had been peering at me round corners and from gateways. Since the distressing days which ended in the funeral, I had seen no sign of the tail-coat, and I concluded that it must have been one of the bandits keeping an eye on me while tracking down the man who was now dead.

But shortly after I received a copy of the periodical with my reply in it—or rather, just as I was leaving the office of the editor who had commissioned me to write another article—I had a sensation all over my back that I was being watched. I turned round, but could see no one. Then I raised my eyes to the first floor of a half-ruined house on which the demolition men were working, and there, in a hole gaping in the walls, a dark figure side-stepped and took cover.

It so happened that it was my thirtieth birthday and I had meant to ask some friends to celebrate the end of my third decade. You can imagine what I felt like when now, by daylight, long before the evening, this advance shadow fell across my party.

I went home and up the stairs. My colleague, the man-about-town, was waiting for me in the common room, where we spent the evenings looking at the television programmes.

'Well, shall we have our celebration?'

'I'm not feeling well,' I said. 'We'll have to put it off.'

'Whoever heard of being down in the dumps on a day like this? Thirty is the best age in a man's life.' He presented me with a colourful tie and whispered: 'Come on. I'll drink you under the table. I've got hold of an extraordinary wine.'

While we were talking I noticed a woman, whom I didn't know, sitting at the far end of the room. I had a curious feeling that she must have been waiting for me for a long time. Now she got up and took a step towards me, and I no longer listened to a word my friend was saying. She was about thirty, she had sloping shoulders, and she was very beautiful. Her beauty lay in the small, endearing irregularities of her face and figure and above all in her sad and open look. When she spoke the same beauty echoed in her low-pitched, gentle voice.

I thought at once of that other golden grain of sand which had once, long, long ago, slipped through the hour-glass; it lay forgotten, non-existent, while this new moment advanced upon me.

'I was asked to hand this over to you for your birthday,' she said with a detached politeness, putting the heavy watch on its steel chain into my hand. 'And also this.' She took an envelope out of her bag.

'From him?'

'Yes.'

I wondered if I could ask her if the man who was now dead had known true love, such as can be neither bought nor stolen—had there been this between them? But, before I could say anything, she read the question in my face and put up her hand to stop me.

'Yes, there was, there was,' she whispered. 'And is. And will be. But he was never sure. . . . I played a game with him. Do you understand? And when they

26

let me speak to him at the hospital I went on shouting for an hour, "Yes, yes, yes," but he couldn't hear.'

I bowed my head. My poor friend! I, of all people, understood.

I put the watch into my pocket, saw my visitor to the front door, and came back.

'She's the one,' the man-about-town said softly. 'the one who used to come and see the bandit. But she didn't recognize me. She never saw anything. If you stood in her way she'd come straight on as if she thought she could walk through you. Blind with love,' he laughed. 'But she's seen you. You'd better look out.'

I went into my room and slit the envelope.

You will receive this letter if I am killed, wrote my dead colleague. *You have great gifts. I am writing to you because you know more about me than the others, and you may come to have a better sense of time. Life is given to us only once and we must gulp it down in great draughts, without stopping for breath. We must seize on whatever has the greatest value. I have already spoken of what that is. Not gold or finery. I hope that you will live to experience great happiness. Remember the dark continent where millions of people live. May the day you get this letter be the day of your real birth. . . .*

Struck by a happy thought as though by lightning, I stopped reading. 'I am luckier than he is,' I thought. 'I still have half my life ahead of me, perhaps even two-thirds. I needn't hurry. There's time for everything.'

At this moment, something dark and solid blocked my window. I thought that workmen must be painting the house and had pulled their ladder up to the third floor. Turning the page, I went up to the window, closer to the light. 'But what would painters be doing

27

outside at this time of year?' it suddenly occurred to me. I looked up and started violently. Sitting on the iron ledge outside the window was an enormous owl with fuzzy ears and long grey side-whiskers; oddest of all, it looked out of shape, almost like a primitive sculpture. It was my owl. For the first time I saw it in the flesh. I waved the letter at it and said 'Shoo,' but this had not the slightest effect on it.

A deeply wounding explanation struck me with such pain and terror that I broke into a sweat. Phew! I drew a shuddering breath and wiped my forehead. The owl was sitting motionless in its place, bolt upright, like any other owl. I took another breath, wiped my forehead once again, and tiptoed out. Without remembering how I got there, I found myself outside, in the bitter cold. Where is it I must go? Ah yes, to the clinic, to see my old school friend, the nerve specialist. He had a lively and creative mind. He would be interested in my case and take me in hand,

I strode hastily down the avenue filled with lilac evening shadows, and at once heard the sound of something hopping after me. I looked back. A furry ear and one wing stuck out from behind the nearest tree. The owl was as big as I was!

The doctor was busy. For a long time I sat in front of the white door of his consulting room; beyond it I could hear the sound of steady pacing. Finally the door flew open and my friend came out, dressed in his white overall, his white cap pulled down over his eyebrows, looking drawn and pale with overwork and lack of sleep.

'Well. How's it going?' someone shouted from another room.

'Still the same,' he shouted back, his face contracting in a nervous spasm. 'Still no good.'

I got up. The doctor gradually came to; he saw me, recognized me, and held out his hand.

'If this is a social call, you've come at a bad time.'

'It's not a social call.'

'Well, come over here.' He took my hand and looked at my fingertips. 'How old are you?'

'Thirty.'

'I forgot we were the same age. Well, what are you worried about? Is someone after you?'

'If only you knew who. . . . The strangest character. . . . You'll laugh at me.'

'I know. Want me to show you? Come in.'

He took me into his room and led me to the window.

'My owl,' I whispered.

It was sitting outside.

'Not only yours,' said the doctor. 'Mine too. Let me have another look at your hands. Ye-es. . . .'

He walked over to his desk and stood a moment with his back to me. Finally he turned round.

'Sooner or later you'll find out. I might as well tell you now; you've got a year left to live.'

The floor sank under my feet and I would have fallen down if he hadn't caught me and helped me to a chair.

I know that there are people who are not afraid of death; they have nothing to lose. I confess that I shook with terror. Once my job was finished I was ready to die—but not now!

'I don't believe it,' I whispered.

'You'd better get up and run home,' advised the doctor, raising an eyebrow; his manner was tense. 'You've got a whole year ahead of you.'

'I don't believe it.'

'Get out,' he shouted at me suddenly. 'You're stealing my time. I'm ill myself. I've got eighteen months.'

He did, all the same, stop me on my way out and mutter, almost gabbling: 'It's a well-known disease and it's usually people with creative gifts who get it in an acute form. Flabby characters get it mildly and die without noticing.'

'And you haven't discovered anything? . . .'

'We've found out a lot, but we still haven't got a cure. All the same we know a thing or two.' He added these incomprehensible words: 'Anyone who sees the owl clearly is already half saved.'

He banged the door.

'Do I see it clearly? I must look,' I thought.

I stood listening to the silence and at this moment I heard the bandit's heavy, steel-cased watch ticking inside my pocket. It was doing its job, counting out the seconds. I took it out, fitted the ornate key, and wound the spring. It took twenty turns. There—it was wound up for a year.

'I must hurry. I must think of everything,' I told myself. For the first time in my life I was really hurrying, that is to say hurrying coldly and collectedly.

The clear, frosty evening welcomed me with its cheerful lights, its purring traffic, the distant glitter of its stars.

I decided to look at the stars and think. At once it seemed as if the star-filled sky bent over me, drew closer for me to see the grandeur of its infinity.

'Well, all right. The flesh will die. Let it. But the mind, the mind! Will that vanish too?' I closed my eyes.

'I shall not vanish,' said my mind in the darkness. Unlike my feelings, it was calm. 'Think,' said my mind. 'The world of civilized men is several thousand years old. Yet how long do man-made things last? Clothes, furniture, machines, all fall to pieces within a few decades. How then did we accumulate all these things we see around us? Quite simply: we accumulated ideas—the secrets of metal-working, of medicine, of setting bricks with mortar. . . . Burn the books, destroy the secrets of the craftsmen, let years pass by till they are utterly forgotten, and mankind will rediscover the stone axe and start again on the same road. Your son—not even your grandson, but your son—will dig up the cog-wheel you made when you were young and bow before it as if it were a miracle.'

A loud, clear waltz-tune poured from an invisible loud-speaker and flowed over the town. The composer was unknown to me and I did not really hear the tune. I heard no band, no trombones, and no violins—these were the voices of my feelings. And when the melody was taken up by the woodwind I clearly understood that these were my desires locked up and singing in their narrow box, the tight confinement of my short existence.

'You want to live,' said the unknown composer. 'See what they do to you, the few notes I left behind in the world of men a hundred years ago, after my brief and arduous stay among them. In those who are allotted a short life, the love of life burns with a stronger, brighter flame. It is better to desire and not possess than to possess and not desire. I loved life and I pass my love of it on to you.'

He lowered his voice.

'Listen to me now. My own life, short as it was, over-flowed with joy. But what about you? Did anyone ever shake your hand in gratitude—shake it so hard as to jolt your heart out of its place? Has anyone ever looked at you and cried with love?'

I felt stunned. Nothing of the sort had ever happened to me yet. It was true that I had loved, but no one had ever looked at me in such a way. I had

experienced no great friendship, I had earned no gratitude. . . . I bowed my head and ceased to listen to the
music, while the city lights grew dim around me. All
I could hear now was a cheerful ticking: my watch,
the bandit's gift to me, was busily ticking away my life,
my seconds: 'You have all your life ahead of you, a
whole year. You've only just been born. You're youn-
ger than you were before. Hurry, run to where your
work is waiting for you. Friendship, love—everything
you want is there.'

I set off at a run, leapt into a taxi—'Faster, faster,
to the laboratory.' The driver looked round in astonish-
ment as he changed into top gear.

Leaving the taxi waiting, I ran up the stairs. On the
landing, beside the red-hot stove, the old charwoman
sat nodding in her chair. I shook her awake.

'Quick, quick, give me back my papers. Those you
took from me this morning—I gave you a whole
basketful.'

'Fancy you remembering, dearie.'

I gave a groan and poked about among the glowing
cinders.

'I burnt the lot. It made a nice fire. Your papers
are the only ones that burn so well. I even fell asleep,
it got so warm.'

'Tick-tock-tick-tock,' said the bandit's watch inside
my pocket. Gritting my teeth, I went into my work
room, took down case after case of instruments, and
loaded them into the taxi. I had decided to set up a
laboratory at home and work at night. To think that
I could earn the boundless gratitude of my fellow men
and that I hadn't even made a start!

When I came into the common-room, a case of
instruments under each arm, a few regulars were
already sitting before the television set.

'So that's that, we postpone the celebration,' said the man-about-town.

He twiddled the knobs and the legs of football-players flitted across the screen. The viewers stiffened in their chairs, their eyes fixed and as large as saucers. I heard the ticking of my watch and the realization came to me that if the television programme were to continue uninterruptedly for two thousand years these five men would stay exactly as they were now and be preserved for posterity like the lotus seeds.

I shifted several chairs, together with their occupants, out of my way, carried all my instruments into my room and paid off the taxi.

The owl was on its ledge outside the window. I could now look at it calmly. It was well lit by the strong bulb inside the room. Was I seeing it distinctly? I went close up to it and for a few moments we gazed at one another through the glass. Then the owl walked the length of the iron ledge and back (just as an owl does on a tree-branch at the zoo); it bent forward, raised its enormous three-toed foot, yellow as though dipped in wax, and swiftly, like a hen, scratched its beak with its back claw. Then once more it settled down, bolt upright, and fixed me with its two tin-button eyes. I could see my owl distinctly.

I came to myself and hurried to unpack my instruments and set them up. Within five minutes my room was a laboratory glittering with glass and nickel.

'But what can I get done?' I thought. 'I need at least ten years.' I made an effort to remember some, at least, of the ideas which at various times had served to light our stoves. I tried to write them down, but nothing came of it.

'They would have cut down my work by half!' I banged the table with my fist.

Then I saw the bandit's letter, lying on the floor where I had flung it down earlier in the day. The few lines I had left unread were staring at me.

I can help you. Did you understand the story about the bandit? If so, ask the woman who brings you this letter to give you the notebook in which I secretly put down all your ideas—those you have been throwing into the stove for the past two years. I meant to use them, as apparently you didn't need them.

'Where can I find her now?' I shouted, still not reading to the end of the letter. Then I saw the words: *Her telephone number is. . . .*

Within seconds—as in a fairy tale—I was back in the common room where the television viewers sat breathing steadily, sound asleep with their eyes open. I propped the telephone on the shoulder of one of them and dialled the number. It rang several times before I heard her voice.

That moment of my new brief life opened a new chapter. It began with a misunderstanding which arose through my own fault.

'Why don't you pick up the receiver at once?' The words came rushing out before I had time to think how rude they were. 'Where's the notebook? Why didn't you give it to me?'

'You didn't ask me. You didn't even read the letter. It said that if——'

I flew off the handle again: 'It's obvious that time means nothing to you! . . . I'm sorry.'

The telephone was silent.

'Why don't you say something?' I shrieked again. 'The notebook, the notebook.'

'I'm on my way,' replied her warm low voice.

3

WHEN I heard her footsteps I realized that it wasn't only the notebook I was waiting for. From the very moment I had first seen her I was drawn to her as inexorably and unconsciously as a piece of driftwood to a distant waterfall. Could it be that another golden grain of sand was on the point of slipping through the hour-glass? 'Well, let it,' I thought. 'None of this exists for me any longer. . . . Lovely women want to be pursued and courted stubbornly and for a long time. And they are right. And no one has more right to it than you who have not forgotten shouting yes, yes, yes to a dying man. And are you likely to forget him? Is my commonplace image likely to drive out of your memory that improbable, exotic man with his borrowed face? No, so far as love goes, I am dead, I don't exist.'

At this point the door opened and she walked in— small, with her sloping shoulders and her tranquil beauty. 'I love you,' shouted every living fibre of my being. I realized that the childhood of my new life was over, I had reached adolescence. But a dry tap on the window cooled my ardour. I didn't even have to look to know what it was.

With hardly a greeting I snatched the notebook from her hand, turned my back on her, and opened it. It was full of drawings, sketches, calculations—those I had been scattering and burning all these past few years. I turned the pages. Wonderful! Now it would need eight years, not ten, to do the job. By working at home as well as at the Institute I could save another two. I would follow several lines of research at once. I would work day and night.

'Why are you in such a hurry?' asked the woman, as I hastily connected wires and switched plugs.

'I have very little time——' I broke off. 'Life is short and there's a lot to do. I'm getting on with it.'

I set all my apparatus going; cheerful lights shone in the retorts, transparent fluids bubbled in glass tubes and rare earths melted in the crucibles.

The owl slept on its ledge, its head tucked under a wing. I decided to resolve one lingering doubt.

'What's that outside the window?' I asked the woman, pointing to the owl. At these words the huge bird raised its head, stared out of the yellow lenses of its eyes, and blinked rapidly several times. The woman went up to the window, put her face against it, and held her hands on either side to shut out the light.

'There's no one there,' she smiled, and broke off. Looking at me intently, she bit her lip as though struck by some discovery. 'There's no one,' she said again. 'Did you see anyone? Are you being followed?'

'There can't be anyone if you say there isn't,' I evaded.

But now she questioned me in her turn and it was I who was surprised and baffled.

'Why have you changed your room?' she asked.

I looked at her, startled, but said nothing: I was already spellbound by my new discipline. I turned the handle of my old adding machine and made a calculation. The woman was still watching me.

Neither of us spoke for about an hour. At last she couldn't bear it any longer, and laughed softly.

'You might at least tell me what all the hurry is about.'

'What it's about? He—you know who I mean—he must have told you.'

'Yes, he told me.'

'Well, that's why I'm in a hurry too. I've lived a whole life and I haven't done a thing. And yet there's something I could do for people. I'll never feel I've got a foothold on the earth until someone shakes my hand in gratitude—shakes it so hard as to jolt my heart out of its place. Now I'm working for him. The day he comes, I'll be happy.'

She must have liked what I said. She remained silent for a while, then she began again.

'Why do you waste time? It's so unlike you. You know you've got a brand-new calculating machine with all the latest improvements.'

That was news. What could she be talking about? Once again I made no reply. She took my hand and led me to the door.

'What is it now?' I stopped.

'Don't waste time,' she said, mimicking my tones. 'Don't worry, I'll help you to save time.'

She took me to a room on another floor—the one my unusual friend, the bandit, had occupied until a month before—unlocked it, switched on the light, and turned away from me, hiding a smile. As for me, I frankly shone with pleasure: the room was full of the most recent and expensive instruments—exactly those I needed. I looked them over and moved them round and forgot all about her.

'Aren't you ashamed of yourself?' I suddenly heard

her voice. 'Why do you pretend you've never seen them?'

There it was again.

'What do you mean?' I asked her sharply.

'Well, you must have been to see your friend now and again,' she replied evasively. 'Perhaps you've never seen this either?'

There was an unfamiliar plant with a large flower growing in a glass tank on the window-sill. She showed it to me as if setting me a test. All at once I remembered.

'It's a lotus. Grown from a seed which lay in a tomb for two——'

'Right,' she said triumphantly. 'You get full marks. And what about this?'

She handed me a calculating machine of the latest model, the kind I hadn't even dared to dream about. It could do the work of a whole roomful of assistants working with the old machines.

'May I take this?' It was beyond me not to ask.

'You're wasting time.' She raised her voice in imitation of my tone or perhaps the bandit's. 'Yes, yes, yes. It's all yours. All the instruments. And even the lotus.'

I had the feeling that something had annoyed her.

'Oh well, of course,' she said after a while, as though thinking aloud. 'You change your face, your voice, then you have to change your room so that nobody should know or tell. . . . You even change your friends. . . .'

If only I had listened at the time. But, as I have already said, I was completely dominated by the new set of rules which had given a new direction to all my thoughts. I paid no attention to her chatter.

4

IN A single night I made a great leap forward. I was sure now that my early assumptions had been correct. If I could go on at this rate I would get my first result within eight months, and then I could get the whole department to co-operate. The sceptics would be silenced.

Next morning, oblivious to all around me and full of the most joyful hopes, I walked to the laboratory. A blast of talk and laughter met me as I came in. It appeared that my perennial opponent, S, had already printed his reply.

'There's efficiency for you!' the boss exclaimed ironically, and in the circle of my supporters gusts of menacingly cheerful noise rose and fell at his every word.

They all stood round my desk, the boss splitting his sides with laughter; the only figure missing from the picture was the scribe, a pen behind the ear, that is to say, myself.

'Well, brave warrior, it's up to you now,' said the Director, putting the cutting on my desk.

I astounded them by not even bothering to read S, who now struck me as merely a naïve and harmless eccentric. The thought of him no longer stirred me; something else had fired my blood. I brushed him off like a mosquito. I may as well say now that S continued for a long time to write articles for my especial benefit. In one footnote he said that I had taken refuge in shamefaced silence, in others that I had taken a vow of silence, that I had evaded the issue, that I was hiding my head in the sand like an ostrich. He flapped his wings and crowed like a cockerel, hoping that his challenge would be taken up and the fight continued.

Seeing me push the cutting to one side, my colleagues exchanged glances.

'Are you feeling all right?' asked the man-about-town. 'Just look at that, boys. I don't believe he's shaved! And he's dumped his coat on his chair! And two buttons from his coat are missing! Well, well, what d'you make of that? I believe he's a changeling. He's a bit like what's-his-name . . . the man who used to sit next to him.'

He looked significantly at the bandit's empty desk.

It was true that my character had changed sharply. I was a different man. I had stopped playing the great scientist, I no longer spoke in a well-modulated voice, I no longer fussed and cooed over trivial questions. I rushed on in a sort of feverish daze. I had an avid hunger for life and the oddest thing was that my idea of pleasure had completely changed.

What was it that now gave me joy? I gazed ceaselessly at *her*. She had settled in my room, moved in her camp-bed, and assisted me in my experiments day and night. I have no idea when she managed to sleep. I delighted in looking at her as she sat at her table, in watching the angle of her head as she bent over her work like a mother bending to her child.

And looking at the line of head, neck, and sloping shoulder, at this gentle, softly curving arc by which alone I would always have known her, I longed for her to turn and look at me. Guessing my silent plea, she turned and looked, her chin on her shoulder. But, each time, some still-unanswered question stirred in her, and after watching me intently for a moment she would go back to her work.

She decided to set me one more test. We had made it a rule that, whenever we had an hour or two of leisure, we would visit a gallery or go to hear a concert or an opera. One evening, after setting up the apparatus and switching on the current, she took me by the arm and said:

'We have a whole hour with nothing to do. Will you make me a present of it?'

I thought it over.

'Very well.'

We went out. She led me down a street and turned into a dark, tree-lined avenue.

Suddenly she turned and said, addressing me not as 'you' but, familiarly, as 'thou':

'You *must* remember this path.'

I'd had quite enough of it all and I was annoyed. I said:

'It's right that we should call each other "thou", it's high time. But I must ask you to stop playing this guessing game. You've been doing it for two months and I'm completely in the dark. It wastes our time.'

'Why are you always in such a hurry?'

Just then, in shadow beyond the pool of light thrown by a street lamp, I saw the dark shape of my owl; its eyes gleamed and blinked. I stopped. I meant to point them out to my companion, then I remembered that she would see nothing.

'Why am I in a hurry?' I made up my mind to tell her. 'Because I've got less than a year to live.' My words moved her. It was as if they were all she needed for an

41

outburst. She turned, facing me, and cupped my chin in her hands. Her eyes, so close to mine, were full of tears.

'If you're sure of that, why must we have secrets from each other?' she whispered.

Before I could open my mouth, she put her finger on my lips.

'It's *you*, my dear, I know it's you.'

At last I understood.

'You think that I am . . . he?'

'Don't torture me any more. Remember last time, how you tried to hide from me. Why are you punishing me?'

'But I'm somebody quite different,' I shouted. 'Look, my hair is different, my face is different. I haven't changed them. I have no scars, no stitches.'

'There were no scars or stitches then, either, but I guessed all the same. I knew at once. Tell me, when I came and brought you the letter and the watch, why did you change colour and ask me if we had loved each other? You were very anxious to know. I saw through your trick at once—it was too simple.' She laughed. 'I was so happy you asked.'

'I'll soon be really parting from you,' I said.

'We'll never part. Even if you run away from me again, even if you change your height as well as your face, even then I'll find you.'

'I have less than a year to live. That's certain.'

'I don't believe it. You've been saying it for years.'

'It was he who said it,' I reminded her, 'and he was killed.'

'He wasn't. You are so clever, you thought of everything. You arranged for all your things to be handed over to your double—to yourself. Oh, you're cunning! They'll never get you. . . .'

'Oh God! What nonsense!'

I suppose the other used to cut her short in the same way. It made her laugh.

'I won't talk about it again. You didn't like it then, either. I really won't. I like you even better now. You're gentler, and you have a good smile. You speak so well about the man who is to come. . . . I've wasted so much time! Why did I tease you, as if I were a girl in my teens? Shall I shout again that word you so much wanted me to say? Yes! Yes! D'you hear now? Tell me you can hear me. Shout it.'

'I hear you,' I whispered. I could no longer struggle against the current. The driftwood rushed swiftly towards the waterfall. 'Which do you love most?' I asked, 'The one who died, or the one who is here now?'

'The one who is here.'

I was loved. I could see her eyes. I had only to turn my head a little to the right and I could see them shining with tears.

And so I took the place of the bandit who had left us. I was no longer an adolescent, I had grown up.

5

THE doctor's forecast had been correct. One bright summer day, five or six months after I had seen him, I knew for certain that I was ill; I could hardly keep on my feet.

Guiltily I looked at my quiet, distraught love. I said:

'You know, darling, I think I'll lie down. You take charge while I'm in bed. Will you turn on the wireless?'

She turned it on and immediately we heard—now loud and booming, now fading in the crackle of magnetic storms—the voice of the dark continent. Over there they were hard at work, mining coal and growing cabbages by artificial light.

'We'll have to work still harder,' I said. 'We've got to hurry.'

The boiling liquids in the test-tubes ran still faster, the lights glowed brighter.

September was rainy. We finished one experiment. I lay in bed so weak that I couldn't raise my head.

'Open the first of the lead containers,' I said.

She took off the seal.

'It's a dud,' I heard her say softly. 'All there is inside is a little glowing cinder.'

'No it's not a dud,' I said calmly, 'it's only a variant. Everything is taken care of in the other two experi-

ments. The cinder will do for a demonstration. . . .
Get hold of the others. . . . Get the boss. . . .'

They tiptoed in as people do on entering a sick room.
I had never let them in before, and now, as they saw
the room arranged as a laboratory, they stopped and
looked round. They did not know what to make of it;
everything surprised them—the calculations scribbled
on the walls, the scratched furniture (I made notes on
it with a nail) as well as the glitter of the instruments
which gave off a faint warmth.

Then they saw me. My appearance must have
shocked them, for they became even more subdued.
Only the man-about-town, who could not take his eyes
off my companion, whispered something to the chief.

'Tell them,' I said to her.

She spoke about our work for ten minutes, like a
trained scientist, and showed them the cinder which
gave no signs of going out.

The cinder impressed them all, particularly the
Director. He was the first to come and shake me
solemnly by the hand. After that they all rushed forward noisily, grabbing my weak hands and shaking
them—and I felt as if at any moment they would jolt
my heart out of its place.

'From this day on we all work together,' said the
chief. 'I'm putting the whole team on to it.'

Two of them remained on duty in my room day
and night, while the laboratory reported daily by
telephone. Thus we made swift progress.

On a cold December day my companion removed
the second of the lead seals in the presence of the
Director.

'Another dud,' she told him in a low voice. 'It's
even worse this time. The cinder is quite black.'

45

I overheard them.

'I've made allowance for this failure as well,' I said, scarcely able to move my lips. 'Get on with the work. Hurry!'

My hearing had become very sharp. I heard the Director whispering, his hand before his mouth: 'A third failure will kill him.' He added aloud: 'Hmm.... I think I'll take this lot over to the laboratory. We'll carry out the third experiment there—we have better facilities.'

'Go ahead,' I said.

And so my wife and I were left alone in the quiet, empty room—we two and the owl. A few days earlier, when the window was half open, the owl had managed to squeeze into the room; it now slept on the window-sill or walked about under the desk, pecking at the floor. My wife—she had every right to be called my wife—sat beside me, and we talked softly, remembering our brief youth.

Three or four days later I felt worse; I asked her to throw the window open.

'Darling! It's bitterly cold. Must I?'

'Open it, open it,' I whispered.

She went up to the window.

'What *is* this? Spring in December! Can you hear? It's thawing, and there's a fly buzzing on the window-pane!'

'Open it. . . .'

She pushed the window open, then flung it wide —and together with the warm spring breeze an astonishingly pleasant distant music filled the room. It flowed over the town, now dying away, now rising in great surging waves. I listened, not knowing that it was the vibration of the wires carrying the news to all the world—news of man's victory over cold and darkness. From time to time this music was joined by the solemn, ringing, and receding sound of aeroplanes: they flew over the town bearing their precious freight of spring to the dark continent which had never seen it. None of this I knew, and I felt very ill and at the end of my strength. I lay listening for the sound of footsteps, waiting for my friends to bring me the good news. I was also frightened by the odd behaviour of the owl: it walked about excitedly round my bed, shaking out its feathers and occasionally fluttering its wings. There is nothing more depressing than to take leave of life before the completion of a useful job you have in hand and which depends on you.

Little by little I dropped off to sleep. Voices echoed in the stair-well, doors banged, footsteps scurried, but I heard none of this. The first thing I heard was the voice of my old school friend, the doctor:

'He's still alive.'

As he sat down by my bedside, his shaking fingers were unscrewing a lead capsule.

'Quick, quick, tell me!' I tried to shout.

And shout I did because my illness had left me.

A dazzling drop of light trembled in the doctor's hands, flooding the room with sun. I had known about it a long time, I had often dreamed about it; at the very outset of my experiments I could see it every time I shut my eyes. Now this small bright sun was too strong for my eyes. I got up, swaying weakly. My wife ran to help me, but I waved her back and walked across the room on my own. I even stamped my foot! She leaned back against the wall, radiant and incredulous.

'Thank you, Doctor,' she whispered.

'For what? It was he who conquered his own death, he who found the cure. This light is his.'

Once again the staircase echoed and doors banged. The whole crowd burst into my room—friends, colleagues, strangers. They surrounded me, they shook my hand. The chief pushed his way through.

'So you really did get your measure of time pressed down and running over,' he congratulated me. 'In ancient times your emblem would have been the owl. Do you remember?—you once suggested it was a hieroglyph.'

'Do you know, I believe it's true—there's some supporting evidence, 'I said. 'It's true,' I thought. 'I've lived a whole lifetime in a year. And how many more such years have I ahead? A great ocean of time.'

Whom was I to thank? I looked at the window-sill, but the owl had gone. Only the lotus blossomed in its glass tank. And outside, far, far away in the pale-blue sky of spring, some large bird winged its way heavily to the horizon.

The sea of time lapped at my feet. I stood on the shore, ready to start life again from the beginning, and, wave after wave, the mysterious future surged towards me and drew me on. 'Tomorrow I'll be sailing on the far side of the horizon.' I felt a little frightened: the owl had never left me for a year and I was used to it. Could I manage without its reminders? Or would this mighty ocean which awaited me turn into a rivulet which I would scarcely notice as I stepped across it?

At this point I remembered the bandit's gift, the watch, and I froze with terror: I could no longer hear its ticking.

I pulled it out. . . . Well, of course! The watch had stopped. A year had passed and it needed winding.

I fitted the ornate key and turned it twenty times. There now, it was going. It was ticking into the New Year.